Miss Polly
and the
Crocodile

Miss Polly
and the
Crocodile

Written and Illustrated by
Felicia Thomas

First published in 2021 by Child's Eye,
Redshank Books

Copyright © Felicia Thomas

The right of Felicia Thomas to be identified as
the authors of this work has been asserted in
accordance with the Copyright, Designs and
Patents Act, 1988.

ISBN 978-1-912969-23-4

A CIP catalogue record for this book is
available from The British Library

Cover and design by Carnegie Book Production

Printed in the UK by Halstan

Redshank Books
Brunel House
Volunteer Way
Faringdon
Oxfordshire
SN7 7YR

Tel: +44 (0)845 873 3837

www.libripublishing.co.uk

For my Mum,
Stephanie Gorgeous Thomas.

Felicia Thomas

Felicia Thomas is an artist who grew up in Kent and moved to County Kerry almost 30 years ago. She lives there with her husband, two dogs and lots of books. She has three grown up children and is also a wedding celebrant.

In 2013 Felicia had an accident that was life changing. She used her hobby of art as rehabilitation and while she was learning to use her hand again, she wrote the beginning of this story.

In addition to supplying gift shops with her art, Felicia has been painting more little characters and is busy writing stories about them. The world of Miss Polly seems certain to grow!

Contents

Chapter One

Once upon a time there was a young witch who lived in the Kingdom of Loopaloo. She was thoroughly spoilt, demanded that everyone do what she wanted them to, and was just not very nice. She was also the Princess of Loopaloo which meant that her Dad was the King and that is pretty much how she got away with being so mean.

Her Dad was very old and grumpy, they shared the same disposition. As he really didn't like listening to his daughter's giant tantrums, he just gave in to her all the time. What the king did like was eating toast, it was the only thing that made him less grumpy. Actually, it wasn't the toast that cheered him up, it was what he could spread on it. Jam, honey, marmalade, he was always demanding the cook come up with new flavours.

This princess had decided at a very young age that school was boring; learning was boring and therefore she did absolutely no work. She was a princess, why should she? She had servants to do her homework for her, if she didn't get an 'A' she threw the servant into the moat, and that is how her education progressed all through school.

This was all very well but it meant that she wasn't the cleverest child; she could read and write, and she had learnt to count so she could count her stacks of money. Did she learn any of her magic spells? No, that was too hard, she learnt very little, and as we all know, a little knowledge is a dangerous thing...

She spent her time taking up new hobbies (and then giving them up as soon as any hard work might be required), lounging around eating cake (and not sharing it with anyone) and complaining that her life was 'so hard'.

One day the king was woken by the sound of his daughter screaming. He got his old aching bones out of bed and hobbled to the princess's room to see what was wrong.

The princess was having a full-blown tantrum, her face was almost purple from all the screaming. When he opened the door, he saw dresses and shoes and even a hairbrush flying through the air. The poor maid was used to this behaviour, she had become very good at diving under the bed. Today's tantrum had been caused by the fact that it was Tuesday and the princess wanted it to be Saturday.

The king watched his daughter scream and throw things and decided there and then that he could no longer tolerate her behaviour. He was getting a headache and that made him even grumpier.

He called everyone into the great hall and announced that he was going to pursue his dream of searching the world for new toast toppings.

He had heard of a lovely pickled onion and banana marmalade in a distant land and that was to be the first destination. No one could know where this would lead but the king wanted to go, and a little thing like running his kingdom wasn't going to stop him. (You can see where the princess got her attitude from.)

The people who lived in Loopaloo were very sorry when they heard this news. They didn't mind the king having a holiday, but this adventure could take years and the spoilt princess would be ruling the kingdom while he was gone!

On her first day in charge the princess was shown her list of duties and was horrified to discover she didn't know how to do any of them. She had very little magic to help her but instead of learning, it seemed easier to find someone to do it for her. She called her servants to the palace and demanded (yes, demanded, asking nicely was not how she did business) to know who was the cleverest person in the land.

Now the servants didn't want to name anyone. Whoever got the job would never get a moment's rest, but when the princess threatened to sing all day, they had little choice but to suggest someone (her singing was atrocious).

Chapter Two

In the old part of town lived the Inventor. He spent most of his time fixing things for the town's people or coming up with new gadgets to make life easier for everyone. After much discussion the servants thought he might be the man for the job — so the princess sent for him.

The princess decided they would make a brilliant team. What with the Inventor's brains and her shouting loudly at people to do things for her — it seemed she would rule the kingdom with ease. When the princess told the Inventor of her plan, he declined to have anything to do with it. 'No thank you,' was all he would say.

At first, she was confused; no one had ever refused to do what she wanted them to before. Then she got cross and said, 'If you don't do it, I will hold my breath until I go blue!' The Inventor sat down and patiently waited for her to go blue... but she gave up very quickly and hadn't even begun to change colour.

Eventually she decided to try and bribe him. She asked the local shopkeeper what the Inventor's favourite sweets were. She bought a whole wheelbarrow full of liquorice allsorts to present to him... but the Inventor still did not want to help her.

When she heard this the princess was furious – if he wouldn't help her voluntarily, she would cast a spell to make him do it. She stomped off to her bedroom to search for her spell book. When she had thrown all of the books from the bookshelf onto the floor, she noticed the spell book poking out from under her bed. It was covered in a thick coating of dust and tucked inside the front cover was her old wand.

Huffing and puffing she stomped back to the great hall where all of the palace servants and the Inventor were waiting. She opened the book, read the spell, lifted her wand and in a terrible rage she cast a wicked spell!

There was a great puff of smoke, a loud bang and then silence. When the smoke cleared there was no sign of the Inventor. There, where he had been standing was a Crocodile... but not an ordinary Crocodile. The princess had been so full of meanness when she cast the spell that turning him into an ordinary Crocodile wasn't enough for her.

The Crocodile that stood on the floor was a sorry sight indeed. He had a shock of purple hair standing up on his head and on his feet were three wellington boots. None of these boots matched, one was yellow and black stripes, one was plain black, and one was red with white spots. On his fourth foot was an old roller skate that had squeaky wheels — in fact the only way you could tell it was the Inventor was because he was still wearing his glasses!

The poor Inventor was miserable; he couldn't go home as his little legs wouldn't manage the stairs, so he clomped and squeaked off to the park in the town where there was a pond he could hide in.

At first people felt sorry for him; they came to visit regularly and tell him the news.

Of course, people tried to reverse the spell, but nothing worked. It seemed only the princess would be able to remove it.

The Crocodile enjoyed these visits from his friends, but as time passed the visits got fewer and fewer until hardly anyone came. One day his friend came to tell him some news. The princess had been so impressed when the spell she put on the Inventor worked that she had attempted another.

Being rather vain she had attempted to make herself more beautiful. Unfortunately, it had gone horribly wrong, and she was now refusing to come out of her room until she found a spell to undo the damage.

The Inventor realised the princess could never remove his spell; he would be a Crocodile forever. He hadn't actually thought she was clever enough to reverse it but now he had proof — if her own spell had gone so horribly wrong what chance did he have?

So, he settled into a life of swimming, warming himself in the sun and repeating mathematical formulae in his head to keep his brain active.

The people who knew the Inventor got older and they didn't remember to tell their children the story. The children just saw a Crocodile — a funny, purple-haired Crocodile with glasses who couldn't move very well because of his squeaky wheels and wellington boots. Everyone knows that people can be afraid of things they don't understand. So, when a group of children met the Crocodile, they were afraid of him. These were not kind children; it was the local bully and her gang.

They thought it would be great entertainment to throw stones at him and call him names. Of course, this made the Crocodile very angry and upset. The stones hurt him and when the gang made fun of him it hurt his feelings. Eventually the Inventor shied away from meeting people completely, he was afraid of them now and got grumpier and grumpier by the day.

Chapter Three

Loopaloo is a very pretty little town. If you look in one direction you can see the mountains and forests, and in the other you look down towards the sea. There are lots of little cobbled streets, the houses are painted in pretty colours, and everyone knows everyone else.

There, in a little lane by the harbour, is a tea shop. It is a lovely old stone building; it has a red roof with a very wonky chimney and a matching red door. Over the door is a sign that says, 'The Cobweb Tea Shop'. This is where Miss Polly lives.

Many years before, the wind had blown Miss Polly Dolly into the town, and as yet, had not blown her away again.

She had floated down from the sky one autumn day with her wand, a small bag and a very peculiar looking bird cage.

She settled into the town very nicely, made friends and before long people were noticing that if they ate Miss Polly's cake their problems seemed to disappear.

Everyone in town liked to go to Miss Polly's tea shop for tea and cake and a chat. Mrs Adams (who had been a friend of Miss Polly's for a long time) helped in the kitchen. Between the two of them they made sure the kettle was always boiled and the cakes were always ready. Mrs Adams didn't sleep very much; she spent a lot of nights practising new recipes. This made for a delicious smell floating through the

town every morning. Today it was pear and blackberry cake.

Miss Polly was very good at magic; she was wise and friendly, and the townsfolk liked her very well.

Inside the tea shop is a lovely place to be. There is a big pot-bellied stove, so it is very cosy and no matter how many people come in, there are always just enough tables and chairs. The townsfolk would come in and spend hours drinking tea and daydreaming. Sometimes they would tell Miss Polly about a problem they were having and she would go to the shelf and take down her big spell book. This spell book seemed to have a cure for everything. Miss Polly and Mrs Adams would whip up a recipe, add some magic and everything would be well again. Mrs Adams always said the best magical ingredient was asking for help in the first place.

The walls of the tea shop are papered with old maps and knitting patterns, poems and recipes. You can sit with your tea and knit a jumper from a pattern on the wall. The only problem is that the part for the sleeves is glued to the wall, so a lot of sleeveless pullovers have been made. On the counter, next to the cake stands, sits the birdcage that Miss Polly brought with her.

This particular one is black, shaped like a dome and has a big ring on top for carrying it. The ring is threaded with ribbons and string and the odd paper aeroplane. Hanging

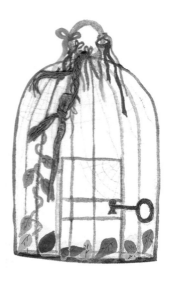

from one of these ribbons is Mrs Adams' magic wand. On the front of the cage is a small door with a keyhole. It has a big black key sticking out of it, but it is rarely locked.

Inside the cage is tricky to see, as most of the cage is covered in cobwebs. If you look at the floor of the cage you can see scraps of silk, wool, feathers and leaves that make a most comfortable bed for the occupant. This is where Mrs Adams lives. She is about the size of a saucer; she is black, hairy and has a selection of leg warmers in various coloured stripes. She is wearing red and white stripes today, eight of them (leg warmers that is, not stripes) – eight of them because Mrs Adams is a spider.

Now that the summer had arrived, Miss Polly's niece Mabel had come to stay for the school holidays.

Mabel was a quiet, shy little thing but she loved staying with her aunt and Mrs Adams — there were always great games to play and both magic and cake to be made in the tea shop. She didn't know any other children in Loopaloo but was very happy in her own company if she wasn't helping her aunt.

Chapter Four

Back at the castle, the princess was getting desperate
for a cure to her spell. She had tried everything she knew
(which wasn't very much) but nothing had worked. The sun
was shining and she wanted to be outside, but wouldn't
leave her room. As we know, the princess was used to
getting her own way all of the time, and this did not suit
her plans at all!

She overheard her maid and the gardener talking about Miss Polly's tea shop. The maid said that eating a piece of cake had cured her backache, whilst the gardener said he had a slice of strawberry tart and now his strawberries had grown to twice the normal size and were the sweetest they had ever been!

So, the princess sent her maid into the tea shop in search of a cure. When she got there Mrs Adams was sitting on the counter knitting a new set of legwarmers. She gave the maid a big welcoming smile and offered her a cup of tea.

The maid explained the problem, but Mrs Adams shook her head. 'I'm afraid I cannot help you. The person who needs the help must ask for it themselves.'

The maid knew that the princess would throw another tantrum when she heard this. As she was in no hurry to face that, she sat down and had a cup of tea and a scone.

Somehow after eating the scone with lashings of jam and cream she felt much calmer about facing the princess.

You can imagine how badly the princess took this news. She flew into a fury. How dare Mrs Adams *not* help her!

After she had thrown all of her shoes at the wall, she calmed down a little and thought of a very cunning plan. She would have someone steal the spell book for her — that would teach Miss Polly and Mrs Adams a lesson.

The next morning Mabel was watering the flowers outside the tea shop when a group of children arrived. They asked Mabel if she wanted to play with them at the park. Mabel, being shy, wasn't sure she wanted to go but didn't want to seem rude. She left a note on the counter to tell her aunt and Mrs Adams where she had gone and said she would be back for lunch.

Mabel discovered that her instincts were right, she didn't like these girls. The leader of the gang was called Hilda Blogs (a tall girl with particularly large feet) and she liked to shout mean things at all the people they met. The

rest of the girls seemed to go along with whatever Hilda said. Mabel was glad when it was lunchtime, so she had an excuse to leave.

The next day they called for Mabel again — this time they wanted to hang out at the tea shop. Hilda kept asking Mabel about her aunt's spell book and the cakes she made. This seemed very odd to Mabel, she wondered why Hilda was so interested. She didn't tell her aunt about this because she didn't want to make a fuss, but poor Mabel was a bit afraid of these bullies.

Hilda rather liked being the chief bully, it meant everyone did what she wanted. The princess was her very distant cousin and they shared many of the same characteristics (which is not something to be proud of). Hilda liked to tell people she was related to royalty but got very cross if they reminded her what happened to the princess when she didn't learn her spells properly.

When Mrs Adams heard Hilda bragging about her cousin she understood at once what was happening. Hilda was trying to scare Mabel into giving her the spell book so the princess could find a cure! Mrs Adams had a quiet word with Miss Polly, and they came up with a plan. If the princess had simply come to them herself to ask for help, they could have removed the spell. But if she got someone to do it for her, or worse, steal the spell book, whatever spell she tried simply wouldn't work.

Mabel tried to stay away from the gang but the next afternoon they followed her to the park. They found Mabel by the pond; she was lying on her back reading a book.

The Crocodile was lying by the edge of the pond; he had fallen asleep in the sunshine and was snoring gently.

Hilda was in a terrible mood. The princess was furious with her for not getting the spell book and Hilda had decided it was Mabel's fault. She wanted to cause some mischief to pay Mabel back.

As she was far too lazy to do anything for herself, she told Mabel to poke the Crocodile with a stick to see if he would move. Now, Mabel knew this was wrong, she didn't want to hurt the Crocodile, so she tried to be brave.

'I don't want to,' whispered Mabel. Her legs were shaking as much as her voice.

In a flash Hilda was on her feet. She stood very close to Mabel looking down at her with her very red, angry face. 'What did you say?' she bellowed. 'I... I don't want to hurt him...' squeaked Mabel.

'You will do what I tell you to if you know what's good for you!' roared Hilda.

Mabel wasn't quite sure what Hilda meant by that, but it was enough to terrify her. She wished very hard that Miss Polly was there, she always knew what to do.

Fortunately, Miss Polly and Mrs Adams were very good at hearing wishes and sensing when trouble was afoot. They decided that Miss Polly should go and find Mabel while Mrs Adams put their plan in action.

Miss Polly picked up her wand and swished it through the air. There was a pop, a flurry of glitter and Miss Polly was gone.

The Crocodile was still asleep in the sun minding his own business. Mabel felt sick, she really didn't want to do it but the girls were all shouting at her and she was very scared. She thought about running away but knew they would chase her and there was no one else in the park to ask for help.

Mabel didn't know if she was more scared of the bullies or the Crocodile. She knew it was a terrible thing to hurt another creature but thought if she just pretended to hit him then she could run away.

Just as Miss Polly arrived, she saw Mabel running towards the Crocodile with a stick in her hand.

The Crocodile was woken by the sound of the girls laughing and cheering. He turned his head so fast to see what was coming that his glasses fell off. What happened next was a series of very sad events...

The Crocodile couldn't see at all well without his glasses, all he could make out was what looked like a stick coming towards him. (Actually, he couldn't see very well with them

either – no one had thought to bring him to the opticians to get new ones.)

Mabel closed her eyes and tried not to listen to the bullies cheering and laughing.

Just before Mabel reached the Crocodile Miss Polly stepped between them and stretched out her arms to keep them apart...

The Crocodile opened his jaws to bite the stick. He snapped his jaws closed and CRUNCH!!!!

Oh dear, oh dear, oh dear. In all the hullabaloo he had in fact bitten off two of Miss Polly's fingers!

Mabel opened her eyes and stared disbelievingly at her aunt. When the Crocodile realised what he had done he burst into tears; he really hadn't meant to hurt anyone. Hilda and her gang knew they had gone too far this time and they ran away.

Meanwhile, back at the tea shop, Mrs Adams felt a shiver run up her hairy legs which meant that she and her magic were needed elsewhere.

But before she could leave, she had to set a trap. Mrs Adams and Miss Polly were quite sure that the princess was trying to get the spell book by any means. If they were both gone from the teashop it would give the princess a window of opportunity.

Mrs Adams knew she had to go and help Miss Polly, so she did the best thing she could to protect the spell book.

She put the 'Closed' sign on the door and put the spell book into her birdcage. She turned the key in the lock and said a little spell, the cage shone brightly for a second and Mrs Adams was ready to leave.

She held her breath, flicked her wand and transported herself to Miss Polly's side. Immediately she understood what had happened. With a flash of her wand Mrs Adams bandaged Miss Polly's hand and cast a spell so that it would never, ever hurt her. The Crocodile was so ashamed of what he had done, he swam away into the pond and thought he would never again come out.

Mabel was sobbing hysterically; she was so upset that her actions had led to this. Miss Polly assured her that her hand didn't hurt at all and that it would all be fine once they went home for some tea and cake.

When they got back to the tea shop however, things were not as calm as they had left them. They could hear someone shouting and it was coming from the counter. When they went to see what it was, they couldn't help but laugh. Mrs Adams' spell had worked very well indeed.

The princess had been very pleased with herself when she came up with this plan.

First, she had told Hilda to cause such a scene in the park that Miss Polly and Mrs Adams would have to leave the tea shop.

Then she had hidden in the lane beside the shop and waited for them to leave.

Of course, when she made this plan, she had thought one of her servants would do it for her but to her utter horror they had refused. Actually refused! There was no time to delay so she had no choice but to do it herself.

She snuck into the back door of the tea shop and searched the kitchen for the book. On the shelves she found jars of ingredients, books about flowers and places to travel, mixing bowls and cake tins, but no spell book.

When she couldn't find it in the kitchen she started searching behind the counter. There inside the big black birdcage was the book! 'This is so easy,' thought the princess. She reached for the key but as she turned it something strange began to happen. She suddenly felt as if she were floating and everything around her looked unusually large. She felt herself shrinking, and before she knew what was happening, she was locked into the birdcage and the spell book was sitting on the counter. She looked through the bars of the cage with disbelief, this kind of thing did not happen to a princess, especially one who always got her own way. In between roaring for help and crying she thought of all the things she would do to her servants; they were definitely going into the moat after this. Then she remembered that she had fired them all when they wouldn't help her, so now she really was stuck with no one to rescue her.

Miss Polly and Mrs Adams stopped laughing, it wasn't really fair. The princess had never been taught any manners, she had always got what she wanted, she didn't know how to be polite. Now here she was, looking most unfortunate from the spell that went wrong, embarrassed at being caught trying to steal, and the same height as a garden gnome.

They waved their wands, and the princess was standing on the floor in front of them, back to her usual size. She was so relieved to be out of the cage that she almost thanked them but remembered just in time that she didn't do that.

'I want you to reverse this spell,' she shouted. 'I want you to reverse it right now!' and she stamped her foot.

Miss Polly and Mrs Adams thought about it for a second. Although the princess had asked for help, she hadn't said please, and they knew Hilda had been helping her. So, they decided that they would help the princess but not in the way she wanted. Mrs Adams wrote down the spell and the instructions and gave it to the princess; now she had a cure but would have to learn some of her magic lessons before she could complete it.

They asked the princess if she would like to stay for tea, but she took the spell and barged out of the door. Her face was bright red, and she was more angry than she had ever been. She stomped back up the hill to the castle wondering where she was going to get some new servants from to help her with the spell.

When the princess had gone, Mrs Adams made some tea. She always thought everyone felt better after tea and cake, so they sat down to have some (coffee and walnut, Miss Polly's favourite).

Miss Polly and Mrs Adams asked Mabel lots of questions about the bullies. They asked why she hadn't told them (although they both knew full well how bullies work) and explained that bullies only have power if you give it to them. They were both very proud of Mabel for trying to stand up to them.

'I should have been braver,' sniffed Mabel through her tears.

'Oh, Mabel, you were as brave as you could be! We know you weren't really going to hit the Crocodile. What's done is done, you can't change what has happened, but you can learn from it.'

'We have all done things we regret,' added Mrs Adams, 'But that doesn't make us bad. Every day is a chance to do your best and if you do that, then all is well.'

But Mabel was still crying. She felt so bad about making the Crocodile scared enough to bite someone. They decided that they would go to the pond the very next day to apologise to him.

Chapter Five

So, the next day they set off for the pond and although the sun was shining the Crocodile was nowhere to be seen. They called his name, but he didn't come out. Mabel left a bag of liquorice allsorts and a note saying how sorry she was, that she had learnt her lesson and would never be mean to anyone again.

When he was sure they had left and he felt it was safe, the Crocodile crept quietly out of the water. He found the note, but he couldn't read it because his glasses were still a bit wonky.

The Crocodile remembered Miss Polly; she was always very kind. He decided that he would wait to see if she or Mabel visited again and then he would try to explain that he was once a nice person and not grumpy and mean.

When Mabel arrived the next day, he was waiting for her. They were a little nervous of each other at first. Mabel explained about the bullies and how she knew she was doing something terribly wrong but didn't know how to get out of it. The Crocodile understood; he told her that he

had been watching Hilda and her gang for a long time and knew how mean they were.

'I know you were only doing it because you were scared, and I don't blame you one bit!' he told her.

The Crocodile and Mabel parted as friends and after she straightened his glasses, she promised to visit him whenever she could. Before she left, the Crocodile asked if Miss Polly would come to see him. He felt dreadful about her fingers and wanted to say how sorry he was.

Miss Polly remembered when the Crocodile had been the Inventor; she remembered how clever and funny he was and felt sad for him to be living in a pond with no friends. When she went to visit him, she brought a picnic and a blanket, and they sat together drinking tea. 'I'm so, so sorry,' he said. Miss Polly said she understood how he must feel since he was laughed at and mocked just because he looked different. They talked for a long time about the old days, they laughed about the princess and her laziness and how things had changed for the town. Rumour had it that the princess couldn't find any new servants and her old ones had only gone back when she promised to be nicer. Time would tell if she could actually do it or not.

Miss Polly told the Crocodile people sometimes treated her differently now. They stared at her hand and thought she couldn't do the things she used to do. But she could! She worked hard to learn to use her hand again; she could still bake and knit and use her wand. Her hand may look different, but it was part of her, and she was very happy to still have any fingers at all. Not everyone had a hand like hers — being different made her feel special.

Polly visited the Crocodile every day and they became good friends, he looked forward to her visits greatly. On the Crocodile's birthday Miss Polly arrived with a cake for him, he smiled a big toothy grin and made a wish as he blew out the candles.

Now, since we know that Miss Polly is magic, she was able to hear his wish — he would like a hug, he hadn't had a hug for so many years. Miss Polly bent down and gave him a hug and blew him a magic kiss. Boom!!! There was a flash of light, a puff of smoke and there, standing beside the pond, was the Inventor! His wellingtons were gone,

his squeaky roller skate was gone, and he was back to his usual self, complete with a beard and white laboratory coat.

Miss Polly and the Inventor walked back to the tea shop arm in arm. Mrs Adams and Mabel were there waiting for them. They made a pot of tea, cut the rest of the

strawberry cake, and celebrated the Inventor's birthday and his return to Loopaloo.

Mabel returned home much less shy and couldn't wait to come back each summer. She had learnt a very important lesson and now knew she could always ask for help if she felt scared.

Hilda and her gang kept to themselves for a while but soon they were up to their old tricks. However, they never bothered Mabel again.

Back in the castle, the princess rang the bell for her maid. She thrust a postcard at the maid and said, 'Read this to me, I'm far too tired to do it myself.' The maid raised her eyebrows and looked expectantly at the princess, 'Oh alright then. PLEASE will you read it to me, I'm far too tired to do it myself.' It was a postcard from the king. He said he had found the recipe for pickled onion and banana marmalade, but it had given him an awful tummy ache. He was now in search of tuna fish and gooseberry jam but would be home soon. 'About time,' thought the princess, then she went back to reading her spell book in the hope of achieving Miss Polly's cure before her father got home.

In the Cobweb Tea Shop Mrs Adams continued to bake her delicious magic cakes and knit pullovers. Miss Polly and the Inventor spent their days together happily, but they were quite sure some magic or a new invention would be needed to save the day again soon.

THE END!!!